Random Humiliations

A Collection of Short Erotica

J.W. Richard

Photo Credit: © Can Stock Photo Inc./Votagerix

ISBN-13: 978- 8837849039

Printed in the United States of America.

Forelsket Press • Las Vegas, Nevada

Also by J.W. Richard

Training Wheels
A Tale of Sexual Discovery

Cassie's Conundrum
A Tale of Forbidden Lust

Oral Anxiety
A Woman's Battle with Her Sexual Demons

Crossed Signals
One Couple's Journey of Sexual Discovery

A Cougar Falls
Stunning Consequences

The Roles We Play
A Spank-tacular Tale

You will find that you survive humiliation. And that's an experience of incalculable value.
      – T.S. Eliot

Contents

Caught

It was a typical school day for me. Instead of paying attention to my geometry teacher I tortured myself by constantly glancing at the girl next to me. She had the biggest set of jugs in the class and I was trying to catch a glimpse of her bra through the tiny slit where her blouse strained against the buttons. Of course I had a throbbing boner during the entire class. When the bell finally rang I held my books over my crotch to hide my erection. Such is the life of a tenth grader.

When I got home I did what I do almost every weekday, I checked to see who was home. Luckily no one else was there yet. I figured I had about thirty minutes of solitude, so I went down to the basement. I took my books with me as cover just in case. I tossed them on the sofa and grabbed the Playboy I had stashed under the cushion. I flipped through the pages but I really didn't need any stimulation; I was ready to explode. I opened my pants and took my dick out. I hadn't touched it but it was already throbbing with a glistening bit of precum on the tip. I grabbed the washcloth I kept stashed under the sofa. It was stiff from all the cum stains but it would have to do. I shifted and held the cloth a couple of inches in front of my cock as my other hand wrapped around it and started stroking while aiming at the rag.

After teasing myself all day it only took a couple of strokes before I felt the intensity of the orgasm that was about to unleash itself. I closed my eyes and gasped just as the first volley shot. At the same time I heard a door and the shuffle of footsteps. I opened my eyes and saw my older sister. Where did she come from? She looked my way and quickly turned her head and walked up the stairs. I had dropped the washcloth while still ejaculating. There was semen all over me, the floor, the couch cushions, and even a little on the wall. I was so startled and confused I didn't know what to do.

Did she see me? She had to. Did she realize what I was doing? She must have. I did my best to clean up the mess but I was afraid to go upstairs. What would she say? What should I say? Should I pretend nothing happened? I decided I would go upstairs until someone else came home. Later that night at dinner I sensed her looking at me, or at least I imagined she was. Would she tell anybody? I was so embarrassed.

The week went by and she never said anything so I relaxed. The day after the incident not only did I not jerk off, I was so traumatized I don't remember even having an erection. By the following day, though, the boner was back and I resumed playing with myself, but I was much more cautious and did it in the bathroom with the door locked. I relaxed when she didn't say anything and even behaved normally around me. Maybe she didn't realize what I was doing. Everything was fine…until it wasn't.

The following Saturday I was home alone hanging out in my bedroom watching TV. Everyone was out running errands or otherwise engaged but I had no idea when any of them might be home so I was behaving myself. At one point I heard the front door open with the sound of footsteps following. My door was ajar and there was a soft tap. It was my sister, Kelly.

"We need to talk."

I felt my face flush and knew I must be beet red. "Su…sure."

Kelly walked in and, to my surprise, was followed by her best friend, Maggie. Now I was confused. My first thought was that she was going to lecture me; now I didn't know what was happening. I sat up on the bed and moved so there would be room for them. Kelly sat on the bed and Maggie took the chair in the corner of the room.

"What's up?" I asked.

"About the other day," Kelly began.

I glanced at Maggie and back at Kelly. She saw my confusion.

"She's my witness."

"Witness?"

She nodded. "I want to be sure you don't twist things around."

"I don't understand."

She got to the point. "What were you doing when I saw you?"

"Nothing, I was …"

"Don't lie to me."

I looked at her and looked at Maggie. They were both staring at me intensely. She obviously told Maggie what she had seen and there was no sense lying about it.

"I was playing with myself."

"Playing how?"

Now I started getting angry. "I was jerking off okay? You caught me jerking off!"

"And what happened when I walked in?"

"I came."

"You ejaculated?"

"Yes"

She turned to Maggie. "See? I told you."

Maggie spoke for the first time. "I see, but I think I need more evidence."

Now I was not only royally embarrassed, I was profoundly confused.

Kelly nodded and snapped at me. "Stand up."

Still befuddled, I did as she said.

"Drop your pants."

"What?"

"Why do I have to say everything twice? Drop your pants!"

I did as she said and unbuttoned my jeans and let them drop to the floor.

"Underwear too."

"Huh?"

"Oh for Christ's sake!" Both of her hands grabbed the waistband of my briefs and yanked them down to my ankles. I was extremely embarrassed…yet I had an erection.

"See?" Kelly asked.

Maggie stood in front of me. "Wow, you're right…he is big. But it doesn't prove anything."

The confusion was off the charts. I'm standing with my pants around my ankles in front of my sister and her friend, I have a full-blown erection, and I have absolutely no idea what's going on.

Exactly what is she trying to prove?

Kelly shakes her head. "Okay," she turns toward me and says, "Jerk off."

"What?"

"Do what you were doing the other day – jerk off!"

I grabbed my dick and looked right at them and tugged away. In a few strokes I was ejaculating. They both jumped back when the stream erupted. Most of it landed on a shirt that was on the floor so there wasn't much of a mess.

"Satisfied?" Kelly asked Maggie.

"Yeah that does it. He's guilty."

"Huh?"

Kelly turned to Maggie, "Good, now spank him."

Stunned, I blurted out, "What?"

"You heard me," Kelly said, "get over here."

She pulled the chair away from the wall and

Maggie sat down. My sister pushed me toward Maggie and then sat on the bed to watch. As I lay across Maggie's lap, I felt my dick get erect again. Maggie shifted and moved me a bit, then her hand came down on me.

Whack!

Ow!

Whack!

It was exciting at first but soon began to hurt. My hard-on subsided as she continued to pound my butt. I was looking at my sister as she sat there with a sinister smile as her friend spanked on; I was so humiliated. She finally stopped and pushed me off of her.

"Face the wall," my sister commanded.

I did as she said. The two of them stood behind me. One of them grabbed a butt cheek and squeezed.

OW!

"Nice and red," Kelly said. "That should teach you a good lesson. Now turn around."

I did as she said as the two of them stood with smirks on their faces and hands on their hips as they looked at me and my now deflated penis. I felt like I was ten years old being chastised for being naughty. Exactly, I'm sure, what she wanted.

My sister shook her head. "If I catch you doing that again you'll get another spanking that's even worse."

When she said that, I instantly grew hard. The girls watched as I came to attention, looked at each other, faces aghast, then turned back to me.

"Do you believe this?" Maggie asked.

"No," Kelly replied before turning and walking out of the room.

I smiled and thought about how I would let her catch me next time.

Triple Humiliation

I got my first hand job at the age of fourteen from the girl next door. She was a year younger than me and we had actually 'played doctor' in my garage about eight or so years earlier. We were sitting on the front steps of her house just chatting about random stuff when she brought up that encounter and laughed about it. I laughed along with her and made an off-hand comment about how different that would be now since the 'parts' we were so curious about were a lot different. It was her next comment that got the ball rolling.

Back then there was no internet and what we learned by way of our friends was more misinformation than anything else. Her remark had to do with that early curiosity; she wondered what an older dick looked like because she had never seen one. I had a hard-on as soon as she said that. Of course, at that age I had a perpetual erection and masturbated on a daily basis. That was part of my problem. Since I had several siblings and a pair of ever-present parents there was always someone home, which meant getting off as quickly as possible so I wouldn't get caught. I had trained myself in a way that would cause problems throughout my life.

When Cathy, my neighbor, kept the conversation going by asking if it really grew bigger I offered to show her. She eagerly agreed. We needed to be discreet so I suggested we go to a park down the block that had a wooded area. It only took a few minutes to get there and my erection was straining against my pants the entire time – I was ready to explode.

We headed for a section that was surrounded by trees and had picnic tables to sit on. Fortunately the area was deserted. We picked the most secluded table and sat next to each other on the bench. She couldn't hide her anticipation. I took a quick look around and then lowered my pants; my dick was throbbing. Her eyes went wide and her gaze was fixed on my crotch. She asked if 'stuff' really came out of my penis and I assured her it did. If she wanted to see all she had to do was rub it. She didn't hesitate; her hand wrapped around my cock and tugged on it. I came on the third stroke and she thought it was the coolest thing as I shot a huge load.

She didn't understand that it was not normal to ejaculate so quickly, but I did. From that moment I always had anxiety about premature ejaculation. As a teen, more than once I came in my pants as I was making out with a girl. When I was lucky enough to get a hand job I tried so hard not to cum that it would happen almost instantly. The first time I had intercourse I ejaculated upon entry. The humiliation piled up and the problem grew worse. I had hoped that getting older would calm down my hair trigger, but it didn't.

Salvation arrived in the form of an older woman, the sister of a girl I had recently broken up with. After the breakup she confessed that she always had a crush on me. I was twenty-one at the time and she was thirty-two. She made no bones about what she wanted so we quickly wound up in her bed. I ate her pussy until she had an orgasm. Then she pulled me up to her and it happened – I ejaculated as soon as I entered her. I was humiliated once more but it did not faze her at all. She just pushed me on my back and started sucking on my cum-covered cock. At first I was very sensitive but that quickly passed and I was fully erect again. She then straddled me and rode my dick like a wild woman. I lasted almost five minutes before I ejaculated again. That was astonishing because I had never lasted even a minute during intercourse.

From that moment on my life changed. Before attempting intercourse I made sure that I ejaculated beforehand. If I acted quickly my erection didn't go down and I could maintain control. I would get a hand job, blow job, tittie-fuck, or sometimes discretely ejaculate into the sheets if I was with someone new. It wasn't a total cure because that first load always happened quickly. Girlfriends were okay with it because I had the ability to stay erect and often got it up three or four times. There was one, Lee, who used my issue to humiliate me. This was not necessarily a bad thing. We did a lot of role playing and humiliation factored into it at times. Our role play included spankings and I was sometimes taken over her knee because I came too soon. Our private games were a lot of fun. That is, until they were no longer private. That's when the triple humiliation happened.

The initial humiliation was when we had a number of friends over and she casually mentioned that if I didn't do something correctly I would get 'another' spanking. A couple of the females laughed and I realized she had told them about our games. The night wore on and the wine flowed and we were having a good time. When we were down to two other couples, as we often did, we played cards that night. It was dealer's choice in that whoever was dealing chose the game. The guys often declared the game was strip poker and the women would shoot the idea down. It had become a running joke. This night was different.

When it was Lee's turn *she* declared the game was strip poker. I laughed but the two other women quickly agreed. The guys looked at each other wide-eyed. While the women weren't exactly supermodels, they were certainly attractive and Lee had a fantastic set of tits that the guys certainly admired. The prospect of seeing the women naked was certainly exciting to all of us and we all got along well enough that jealousy shouldn't be an issue.

The rules were established. In each game the five losers would take off one piece of clothing one at a time as the others watched. No shyness was allowed. The overall winner would be the 'master' and the five losers would be his or her 'slaves' for the rest of the evening. The biggest rule was that anyone could refuse an order from the master but when that happened the night was over. This meant people would go along with almost anything to keep the night from ending.

The game started off very well in that I won the first hand. Turned out that would be the only time I would triumph. The wins were somewhat evenly distributed at first and it was exciting to see the other ladies as they stripped down. When one of the guys won all three women had to reveal their breasts. Lee's were certainly the best and the other guys certainly appreciated them though the others were nice as well. However, by that point I was down to my briefs and was the biggest loser. When I lost the next hand as well I had to stand off to the side and strip of my undies as everyone watched. I was fully erect and I could feel the ten eyeballs staring at me. Lee looked at the other women and said, "I told you he had a nice cock." I was pleased and humiliated at the same time.

I was made to stand at the side of the table while the game continued. After the next hand one of the women had to strip off her panties. She was a blond and I was hoping for a blond bush, but she was a shaver. She had to stand next to me as the rest played on. The other two guys lost next and had to strip. It was another boost to the ego when I saw I was bigger than both of them, though not by much. Lee and the other woman were both down to their panties so the next hand would determine the 'master.' Lee wound up winning, which did not surprise me one bit and she would certainly be the best master. The second woman stepped out of her panties but I was disappointed to see another shaver.

We all stood naked while Lee still had her panties on. She walked back and forth looking everyone over. When she finished her quick inspection she stood in front of everyone and stripped off her underwear revealing her thick, black bush. One of the guys blurted out, "Nice!" Lee resumed her inspections, this time squeezing everyone's ass cheeks. She fondled the breast of the other women and the balls of the guys. Then the games really began as Lee started giving commands.

"Guys," Lee ordered, "It's time for boob inspections, check them all out – starting with mine."

The two guys came over to her and fondled her until she said, "Don't be shy, suck on them!" Suck on them they did. We all did the same for the other women as well. This went on for several minutes until Lee ordered a stop. Lee then told the ladies, "Girls, it's time for a dick check." The guys lined up and the women moved down the line, I was last. Lee led the way. She knelt in front of the first guy's erect cock and gently stroked his balls. Then she stroked him a few times before taking him in her mouth for a moment and exclaimed, "Tasty!" She moved on to the next guy as another lady went to the first. The guys loved every minute of this – I was mortified.

Lee moved over to me and made a perfunctory show of inspecting me. She looked up at me with an evil look in her eyes and a sly smile that told me she knew exactly what she was doing. I was about to be humiliated for a second time. She had both women kneel in front of me. I knew all eyes were on me and I fought for control. One of the girls fondled my balls while the other wrapped her had around my cock and tugged. When she did I exploded with cum shooting everywhere. The girls gasped in shock and the guys laughed. I feel the heat as my face turned crimson. Lee just smirked.

Lee stood there in mock horror. "I can't believe you did that! You need to be punished."

"Spank him," cried one girl.

"Yes!" shouted the other.

Lee left the room for a moment and came back holding a racquetball paddle. She grabbed a high-back chair and placed it in the center of the room and sat down.

She looked at me with a wicked grin. "Get your sorry ass over here."

As everyone watched, I sheepishly made my way over and sat across her lap. It was a position I was familiar with. As everyone watched the paddle hit my ass, gentle at first and then with increasing intensity. *Whack! Whack! Whack!* Tears filled my eyes as I tried to bear the pain, but a few cries escaped. After several minutes she stopped and I slowly got up. Everyone was smiling as they looked at me. I thought my humiliation was complete. I was wrong; the third one was about to happen.

Lee sat back in the chair and sighed. "Whew, that was fun but it made me super horny. Show of hands, who wants to eat me?"

Both guys and one of the girls eagerly raised their hands. Lee looked at the girl with the raised and called her over and then asked, "Who wants a blow job?" Both guys raised their hands.

Lee looked at the remaining woman and said, "Go suck one of them off."

As the girl quickly went to the guy who wasn't her husband, Lee looked at me and said, "Go blow the other one."

I was dumbfounded. "But…"

As Lee pulled the first girl in between her legs she said to me, "Just go suck his dick and don't be such a baby."

I looked at him and then his cock. I watched him grow erect as he dropped into a reclining chair and waited for me to come over. I took a deep breath, walked over, and knelt in front of him. I stroked his cock for a brief moment and then took him in my mouth. It felt strange but I soon got used to it. I did the best I could by trying to do it the way I liked it. After a few minutes he started to squirm and moan a little. He tensed up and his legs quivered a little. Then he grunted and a felt a hot stream explode in my mouth. I did my best to swallow it but there was so much and some dribble down my chin. When I was sure he was empty and leaned back and realized everyone had been watching.

After everyone went home I sat in bed with Lee. I told her I couldn't believe what had happened that night. She confessed that she and the girls had planned it for over a month. I was dumbfounded.

"How much of it did you plan?"

"All of it."

"Everything? Even the…"

She laughed. "Yes, even the blowjob."

"I can't believe it."

"Tell me," she asked, "and be honest – is there any part you wish hadn't happened?"

I hesitated for only a second, "No."

"Thought so."

She slid down and gave me a nice, slow blowjob – it lasted a long time.

Moving Day

Andy carried the box into the bedroom and placed it with the others. The move was almost complete but he had worked up quite a sweat. He wiped his brow and took a large swig from the water bottle. Only one more box to go. He went to the truck and was surprised by its weight. He carried it into the house while wondering what was in it.

"You're sweating like a pig, take your shirt off. I'll get you a beer."

He didn't really know her that well, but figured since she suggested it then it was ok. He took off the shirt and used it to wipe the sweat from his body. He felt better standing there wearing only his shorts. She came back and handed him a Sam

Adams. He couldn't help but notice that she looked him up and down.

"What's in that box? It weighs a ton."

"Just a few gadgets," Annetta replied.

Andy drank his beer and sat on the edge of the bed. She rummaged through that last box while he watched. She came out with something that hand a short chain on it attached to a piece of leather that was lined with sheepskin. He had no idea what it was. She came over to him and held it up for him to see.

"Here, let me show you how it works. Hold out your hand."

He did and in one swift move she wrapped it around his right wrist – the one without the beer – and fastened it shut. Before he could protest she took the chain and leaned over the edge of the bed. He heard a metallic click. She plopped on the bed next to him wearing an evil grin. He tugged at the chain and realized he was restrained.

"Cute," he said.

He put down his beer and went to undo the strap. Before he could Annetta produced another restraint and attached it to his left wrist. She pushed him on his back; she was a lot stronger than he thought. She pulled the chain tight and attached it to the other corner of the bed. His arms were fully immobilized and she stood over him admiring her handiwork. She turned away and walked out of the room.

"Hey, this isn't funny! Come back here and untie me!"

She was gone for more than ten minutes before she returned. When she did she was wearing a black, corset-like top, fishnet stockings, and stiletto heels. She had tied her hair back in a ponytail and wore an expression that said she meant business.

Andy didn't say a word. She rummaged through the box again and came up with two more restraints. She secured them around his ankles and then to the bed. He was spread-eagle wearing only his shorts. The ties had some play in them so he wasn't uncomfortable.

"Now you see what's in the box – at least some of it."

"Nice, but enough already – untie me."

"Oh no, we're going to have some fun first."

She came to the side of the bed. Her hand grabbed the elastic of his shorts and tugged. They came down just a little, far enough to expose the top of his black briefs. He didn't think she could go too far, the way he was laying on the bed wouldn't allow her to pull them down much further. She slipped her fingers under the waistband of his underwear and pulled up, then peeked inside.

"You don't shave, that's good – I like the pubes."

She let go and his briefs snapped back in place. She walked to the top of the bed and placed one of her shoes on it a few inches from his face.

"Like my shoes?"

"Very nice."

"Good, now lick them.

"I'm not doing that."

"Don't be naughty or I'll have to punish you. Now lick them, pussy boy!"

He turned his head and lightly touched them with his tongue. She shifted her foot so it was closer.

"Now lick the toes; that's a good boy."

She pulled her shoe off the bed and looked toward his crotch. There was a bulge so she reached over and touched it lightly.

"I guess you liked that. I think it's time to see just what you've got in there."

She went back to the box and pulled out a pair of shears. She quickly cut through the shorts and briefs and pulled them off. His cock was throbbing and she was pleased to see it was circumcised. She looked at it closely without touching it while she fondled his balls a little.

"Nice cock. What is it, about seven inches?"

"Seven and a quarter."

"Mmm, I may have to take it for a ride. First you have other things to do."

Annetta unzipped her corset and exposed her boobs. She brought them over to his mouth, he didn't need any instructions. He sucked one then the other as she moved them back and forth. Her nipples got very hard and she moaned lightly. She backed up and slipped off her black panties.

"See, I don't shave either. I hope you're hungry."

She climbed on the bed and straddled his face. He began to lick her pussy slowly and gradually increased his tempo. He reacted to her moves and varied his speed and pressure. After a few minutes she reversed her position so she could suck his cock while he ate her. She took him in her mouth and worked slowly to bring him along. At the same time she was bucking in his face as she was about to come.

Ahhh, ahhhh, ohhh, ahhgh!

Ughhh, uggh ughhh!

They came together. She took his load in her mouth but didn't swallow. She turned around to face him then opened wide to show him his semen; she brought her mouth to his and kissed him, sharing his cum. Then she climbed back on his face again so he could eat her until he was hard again. When she was close to another orgasm she reached back for his cock and found he was ready. She slid down and slipped his cock inside her soaking wet pussy and started riding him. She bucked herself on his cock until she came again. She paused a moment and then resumed slowly and kept riding until he came again.

She was totally spent. She slid off of him and got off the bed. She was about to remove the restraints when she heard the front door open. Her roommate was home. Rather than close the door or cover up she just stood there. Her roommate stopped and peered into the room as if this was an everyday occurrence.

"I was just about to untie him," Annetta said. "Do you want to go for a ride or have him eat you…or both?"

"Both sounds like a great idea, I'll go get undressed."

Andy sighed. "Oh god!"

The Cock-Tail Party

Lee was preparing hors d'oeuvres for her gathering. Bottles of wine, red and white, were sitting on the table. Chips and dips on several side tables throughout the room. Everything seemed ready for the guests who should be arriving shortly.

"Anything I can help with?"

Lee glanced over her shoulder and looked me up and down.

"You're not wearing that."

I thought I looked fine. "What should I wear?"

Lee shook her head and snickered. "You're not wearing anything."

"*What?*"

"You heard me."

"You said my punishment was that I had to be the server at your party. You didn't say…"

Lee cut me off. "So I left out a detail – now go get undressed. And be sure your pubes are trimmed; they're getting a bit unruly."

Fifteen minutes and a few trimmed pubes later I returned to the kitchen. I knew a couple of the women reasonably well and the others casually, but I was nervous as hell; none of them had ever seen me naked. Lee sat at the counter casually sipping a glass of wine with a look on her face that ratcheted the anxiety level up even more.

Lee looked at me for a moment before speaking. "That's much better. Oh, you will be wearing one thing."

I sighed with relief but it was only a temporary respite. She picked something off the table and tossed it to me. I caught it and looked it over – an elastic strap with some sort of ball attached.

Lee snickered. "It's a ball gag. You, my dear, will not be speaking a word tonight; you will simply take orders from the guests."

My anxiety level increased to Defcon Four. "What…what kind of orders?"

"Oh relax. Drinks, food, clearing plates, that's all – from them anyway. Now me, on the other hand…."

"What…what do you have in mind?"

"Oh I don't want to tell you….something humiliating for sure. After all, you deserve it."

"Why? It's not like I did it on purpose."

Lee shook her head and sipped her wine. "Perhaps not, but it wasn't the first time either."

"Isn't being naked in front of your friends humiliating enough?"

She laughed. "Not by a long shot. Tonight I have something really special in store for you."

With that last statement she got up and left the room, presumably to go change. She let out a wicked laugh as she did so ratcheting my anxiety to Defcon Three. *What wicked humiliation was in store for me?*

I heard a car pull up and my heart started racing. Lee ordered me to stand by the side of bar setup as she opened the door. I couldn't see who it was but I recognized the voice as one of Lee's friends from work, though I didn't remember her name. She was a cute, thirty-something blonde of medium height. A little chubby perhaps, but a pleasant face and a nice rack. She smiled as she looked me up and down.

"Rita," Lee said, "you remember Richard."

"Indeed I do, though not like this!"

"He will be serving us this evening. You want to be sure he's paying attention so squeeze his balls as you place your order. After he serves you tip him by swatting his butt. Oh, one more thing – if he gets an erection give it a hard smack."

Rita grinned and bit her lower lip, "It's going to be a fun evening!"

With that her right hand reached out and cupped my balls and squeezed hard enough that my eyes watered. "Vodka and tonic with a twist, please."

I returned a few minutes later and handed her the drink and received a sharp whack on my ass. Other guests arrived, four in all, and Lee repeated the instructions to each of them. They ranged in age from late twenties to early fifties and I found it interesting that each seemed to have a different style.

The oldest, Melanie, an attractive woman with short hair and a slender body acted as if parties like this were perfectly normal. She gave my scrotum a gentle squeeze as she asked for a glass of white wine. When I returned and handed it to her she gave me a light tap.

Amy was the youngest and seemed to be the most amused. I knew her from a few other gatherings. She was twenty-eight or twenty-nine and worked as a real estate agent. Amy was the athletic type with reddish hair and a finely-tuned body. To sum it up in a word – she was *hot*. Instead of grabbing my nut-sack like the others, she smiled at me and slowly ran her finger tips down by abdomen and over my penis until she reached my balls. Instead of squeezing hard she caressed them gently. I realized she was trying to arouse me – it worked.

As I quickly became erect Amy loudly exclaimed, "Oh look, I think it likes me!"

With that she squeezed very tightly, then released my balls and swiftly gave my penis a very hard slap that hurt like hell. The women howled with laughter; I felt the blood rush to my reddening face as it left my rapidly deflating cock.

"Now get me a beer server-boy…and it better be cold."

I came back with the coldest Sam Adams in the fridge and handed it to her. In return I received the hardest spank of the night so far. Hot or not, I hoped I didn't have to get her too many drinks.

As I was about to go take orders for another round of drinks, it happened. *She* walked in. 'She' being the one friend of Lee's that I had the absolute hots for and one I hoped would be at the party. Tessa was about forty very tall, with dark hair and mysterious, too me, smoky-brown eyes. To say she was well assembled would be an understatement. I fantasized about Lee and I having a threesome with this woman. I imagined what it would be like burying my face in her luscious, dark bush (if she shaved I didn't want to know – it would ruin the fantasy). What really got to me was her voice; it was husky like the actress from the 1950s, Patricia Neal. I could feel myself start to stir just at the sight of her and knew I was in trouble.

Lee explained the procedure to Tessa, who smiled at me as she listened. She stepped closer and grabbed my balls and whispered her request for a margarita in that husky voice and it was all over – I was at full attention.

"Well, look at that! The little fella became quite a big boy."

Lee stepped over a slapped my dick as she spoke to Tessa. "Don't fraternize with the servant."

Tessa laughed while looking at my still-hard cock. "It's not going away," she said as she gave it a rather hard smack of her own. It finally started subsiding as I went to fix her drink. They were all laughing, at my expense of course. As the blender was whirring I could hear Lee talking and my anxiety hit Defcon Two. *Oh don't worry ladies; the best is yet to come.*

I continued serving drinks and receiving smacks. I kept wondering what other humiliation Lee was so excited about. I didn't have to wait much longer. The doorbell rang and Lee went to answer it. As the latest guest stepped in, I immediately felt very self-conscious – it was my cousin Jacqueline. Jackie and I were the same age and spent a lot of time together growing up but not much of late. While I had been humiliated much of the night, at the moment I was truly embarrassed. Jackie seemed amused by my obvious discomfort as Lee explained the procedure to her.

Jackie stepped close to kiss my cheek as a way of saying hello and then, without hesitation, she cupped my balls and squeezed. "Well," she said, "this is quite an incestuous way of asking for a beer."

I went to the kitchen to get a beer and I heard laughter, chatter, and the scraping of furniture on the floor. Lee was arranging the chairs in a semi-circle. I handed Jackie her beer and received the requisite smack on the ass. Whatever Lee was up to, I knew it wasn't good. Lee placed the final chair facing the semi-circle and invited everyone to sit down and indicated that Jackie should be in the chair facing the group. I was instructed to stand off to the side but in everyone's view. I instinctively placed my hands in the fig leaf position covering my cock but Lee quickly nixed that and told me to place them behind my back. It was officially full alert, Defcon One.

"Ladies," Lee began, "It's story time. Jackie has some things to tell us about Richard."

Oh no,…oh god, no!

"Hmm," Jackie started, "how to begin? I guess with some background. We're the same age, almost exactly; I was born two weeks after him. Our parents were sisters and very close, so we spent a lot of time together growing up. Like most very young kids we were quite curious about our bodies. So we did what kids do – we played doctor. I'm not sure who started it but I was just as into it as he was."

She reached over and gave my penis a tug and quickly let go. "This thing fascinated me. I must say, it's grown quite a bit since I last saw it."

Everyone laughed, including me. I wanted her to stop there but knew she wouldn't.

"We played but we really didn't know what we were doing. We just based it on what we experienced with our doctor. Richard developed this fascination, though. I guess it stemmed from the rectal thermometer – he liked for me to stick things in his ass."

"He still does!" Lee blurted out.

I felt hot as my face flushed and everyone laughed; Jackie went on.

"We used pencils, sticks, whatever we could find. We're lucky nothing ever got lost up there. We eventually outgrew that phase and had a normal relationship. That is, until we didn't. Several years later puberty hit and the hormones were raging. I sprouted boobs and Richard wanted to resume playing doctor. Though I was curious, I knew better and we didn't. But boy did he try. He would beg me to show him my tits."

She turned and used her open palm to point toward my penis. "As you can see, this thing isn't exactly small. I would see his hard-on in his pants quite often and wanted to get a good look at it. So that's *my* confession. I debated showing him my tits so I could see his dick, but I was afraid it wouldn't stop there."

She stood up and faced me. "Now I've finally seen your dick, so it's only fair." In one motion she grabbed her shirt and bra, lifting them high. A magnificent set of 36Cs dropped out. "Here are my tits!"

They were truly beautiful. I felt myself quickly getting erect and didn't care. Jackie dropped her shirt and gently gave my cock two gentle taps before smacking it hard. "Put that thing away!"

The group laughed and gave Jackie a round of applause as well. Lee stood up to address the group. "It's time to introduce our next guest."

I was puzzled; there was no one else here. Lee walked toward the guest bedroom and opened the door. "Come join us."

I was looking over my shoulder to see who it was. When she came into my view my heart sank into my gut. My legs actually quivered. If there was a state of alert higher than Defcon One I was there. I couldn't believe Lee would do this – it was my *older sister*!

Kelly was almost four years older than me. I knew what Jackie was going to say, but I had no idea what to expect now. As Kelly walked to the chair she looked at me with amusement. I was far beyond embarrassed.

She turned toward Lee, "I could use a glass of wine."

Lee laughed. "You know what to do."

Kelly looked directly at my cock as her hand very gently cupped my balls. "The last time I touched these I was helping mom change your diaper." She then squeezed them hard, perhaps in sibling revenge for past transgressions, until my eyes watered. "I'll have a glass of red please."

I would have been singing in a falsetto if it wasn't for the ball gag. She squeezed even harder than Amy had. When I returned with her glass she gave my ass a wallop. I knew whatever she had to say wouldn't be good.

Kelly looked at me as she began. "That was quite an interesting story Jackie told; I didn't know all of that, but explains a lot – especially the puberty part."

Uh-oh

She turned back to the women, who sat in rapt attention. "Being almost four years older I was much more aware of things. It was obvious to me when Richard started going through puberty. There were the random whiskers that sprouted of course, but, as Jackie said, that thing isn't exactly small. I would laugh whenever I would spot a boner (that's what we called it then)."

She looked at my dick for a moment before turning back to face the group. "He wasn't exactly discreet though I'm sure he thought he was. You see, I did a lot of the cleaning. He would usually go into the basement when he came home from school. Quite often I would find one of my older brother's Playboy magazines out down there and knew that it was Richard looking at them. Then there was 'the rag'."

Oh, no!

"This thing was so stiff from all of the cum stains. He had to be jerking off every day. So I decided to catch him in the act. The laundry room was in the basement so I planned to burst in on him while he was doing it. The first time I went down there I watched him but didn't have a really good view."

The first time?

"So I made a little hole in the wall so I could see better. I worked to a degree but I was still pretty far away. Then I had an idea. My mother had a pair of opera glasses, like mini-binoculars, so I would use those. That worked much better."

She was spying on me!

"The next time I got to watch I was ready to get a good look. He came downstairs and tossed his books on the table. The he grabbed a magazine from under the sofa and opened it. He unzipped his pants and took out his hard-on. I had never seen one so clearly. He wrapped his hand around it and only had to tug on it two or three times before it started shooting. Man did it shoot; I couldn't believe how much stuff was squirting out of it. What I really couldn't believe was how fast it happened.

Lee called out, "It still does!"

Kelly continued. "Then he cleaned himself up with that rag and went upstairs. I came down again the next day and that's when I caught him in the act. I had my basket of laundry ready. I heard him come down the stairs and toss his books. I peered through the hole and walked out as soon as he had his dick in his hand. I pretended not to see but he was ejaculating like crazy and I could tell he was panicking. I wanted him to wonder whether or not I caught him."

Everyone was laughing. I couldn't believe she had planned the whole thing. I convinced myself that when she walked in on me she didn't realize what I was doing. What else did she know?

When the women quieted down Kelly told them more. "What Jackie said about him wanting to see her tits helps confirm something for me. I often had a feeling that he was trying to see me naked. I don't think he ever did but I know of something else he was doing. He was going through my underwear drawer. I have a certain way of placing things and they would often be moved. So I started counting my panties."

Oh, no! Don't tell them!

"Sure enough, I started missing a pair here and there. So I came up with a way to stop him. One day I wrote a note that said, 'Put them back!' and left it on top of the stack. The next day they were all there and never disappeared again."

Kelly finished the rest of her wine and turned to look up at me. "Tell me, dear brother, what were you doing with them?"

I couldn't answer with the gag on and indicated as much with my facial expression. Her hand reached out and took my balls in her hand, letting them rest gently on her palm.

"Answer me truthfully or I'll squeeze really, really hard. Were you wearing them?"

I shook my head 'no'.

"Were you using them to jerk off?"

I nodded affirmatively.

She let go of my balls. "Thought so."

Lee stood up and addressed the group. "Now we enter the final phase of tonight's festivities."

There's more?

"So, Ladies, what have we learned about Richard? One at a time, Rita?"

"He jerks off a lot," Rita said.

Amy chimed in next, "He cums a lot."

"Not so much anymore," Lee responded.

"He cums fast," Melanie added.

Lee smirked, "Bingo! What else? Tessa?"

"He likes things in his ass."

Lee grabbed Tessa's hand and raised it. "We have a winner!"

My face felt like it was on fire; I could only imagine how red it looked.

Lee asked everyone to take a seat again as she stood in front of them.

"This brings us to why we are here; tonight was about punishing and humiliating Richard. Yes he sometimes cums too fast but it usually isn't a big deal. He gets it up again quickly and really knows how to eat me. However, last week he came too fast and fell asleep. This has been happening too often lately so he needed to be taught a lesson."

Amy asked, "what else are you going to do?'

"Not me, we. As Tessa said, he; likes things in his ass."

My eyes went wide as Lee pulled out a strap-on dildo and set it on the table.

"Each of us is going to take turns with this paddle." Lee held up a wooden, racquet ball paddle. "Then someone is going to fuck him with the strap-on."

Rita spoke up, "Aren't you going to do that."

Lee smiled, "I have a better idea. Tessa, you know he has the hots for you, right?"

"Of course, he's always staring at my boobs."

"Well," Lee said, "I think you should do it."

"It would be my pleasure to pound him."

"His too, I'm sure."

I was told to position myself over a chair in the middle of the room. Each of the guests took turns pounding my ass with the paddle. Five strokes each, the hardest coming from Amy and my sister, Kelly. While I was recovering I watched Tessa take off her pants and start to position the strap-on over her panties. She saw me watching her and stopped. She paused for a moment and smiled at me. Then she pulled off the contraption and removed her panties revealing a black bush that was every bit as luscious as I'd imagined. I was rock-hard in an instant.

"Holy shit, look at that hard-on; he really wants it."

I had no idea who said it; my eyes were glued to Tessa's bush. I followed as she came up behind me. I felt her hand reach behind my head and pull off the gag; what a relief.

"I want to hear you moaning," she said. "Do you hear me?"

"Yes"

"Yes, what?"

"Yes ma'am"

"That's better."

I was facing the chairs with all of the women looking directly at me. Tessa's left hand was on my hip as the fingers of her right were lubing my ass getting me ready. She started moving into position and I could feel the head of the dildo about to penetrate me. I was looking directly into Kelly's eyes.

She grinned at me, "I'm going to enjoy watching this!"

Tessa started pushing her way in slowly. I closed my eyes and let out a gasp as she went all the way in. She started moving in and out, slowly increasing the tempo until she was pounding me at a steady pace. My cock was throbbing.

Tessa's husky voice asked, "You like that?"

"Uh, uh, yes, uh."

"You want more?"

"Yes"

"Yes, what?"

"Yes ma'am, please."

I looked around at the women; every face was glued to mine. I felt like my throbbing cock was ready to explode. I didn't see Lee but soon realized she was standing next to me.

Uh, uh, oh god, uh

Tessa had her hands on my hips thrusting. I looked at Jackie and then Kelly as they stared at me.

Just then Lee's hand grabbed my cock and stroked it causing me to let out a stream bigger than I had in years. It landed on both of them as they howled with laughter.

Tessa slipped out of me and I collapsed in a heap.

Someone yelled, "That was fuckin' hot!"

"Made me horny," added another.

I was on the floor and rolled over onto my back. I watched as Tessa removed the strap-on. Lee came over and whispered something in her ear causing Tessa to nod. She stepped over me, one leg on each side of my head, and lowered herself down until she was inches from my face.

"Eat me"

"Yes, ma'am!"

She lowered her gorgeous bush to my lips.

Humiliation? Oh no, this was heaven!

The Bestie

I was a typical horny teenager, hormones raging and producing semen by the gallons. Having no outlet, I took matters into my own hand on a daily basis. Living with two sisters, one older and one younger, I had to be discrete. I was just sixteen, with my siblings separated by a few years in each direction. Kelly, the older, had sprouted a pretty nice rack and I kept trying to catch a glimpse to no avail. I did check out her bras and panties now and then out of curiosity but that's it.

Now Jen, the younger, was a different story. She was curious about a lot of things and this was long before the internet, so I was her information source. She would often ask me if things her friend told her were true, they generally weren't and I told her as much. One of those times she came to me and said she said she was afraid because she suddenly started growing hair down south. The right thing to do would have just been to tell her it was normal but, as I said, I was a horny teenager (redundant phrasing for sure).

I said, "Show me."

She hesitated at first but complied after I convinced her that it was ok. She dropped her pants to reveal a few little wisps of pubic hair. I took a very close look and even touched them. I reassured her that it was normal and that the little sprouts would soon be joined by an army of follicles. I then tugged my pants down just far enough to reveal my very thick bush but nothing more. She went away satisfied.

A couple of years later she came up to me with her friend wanting me to settle an argument. Remember, this was the age of misinformation that existed long before the internet. Their dispute involved the male penis, something I just happened to have first-hand knowledge of. They had some basic information from what they'd been told in health classes, but mostly they heard things from friends or through the grapevine. I laughed when they told me what they were arguing about. Jen was maintaining that the dick only got hard but her friend, Nancy, argued that it got hard and grew bigger. Apparently Nancy had seen her brother's erection at some point.

"It gets bigger," I said.

Nancy was gloating. "See, I told you."

Jen wasn't having it. "I don't believe you."

What came next was totally unexpected. Jen and Nancy were bickering back and forth when Nancy turned to me and said, "Show her."

"What? I can't do that."

Jen smirked. "See, I told you he was lying."

"I'm not lying. It's just that…"

My sister taunted me, "What's the matter? You chicken?"

"Fine, I'll show you….but only if you'll take your clothes off."

Now Jen resisted. "I'm not taking my clothes off!"

"Now who's chicken?" Nancy said. "I'll take mine off."

Jen relented. "Fine," she looked toward me, "but you go first."

I quickly undid my jeans and dropped them. I instantly started to grow erect as they watched. Nancy smiled as Jen just stared, mouth agape.

"That thing's huge," Nancy said. "My brother's is much smaller."

Jen hadn't said a word; she was just staring at my cock.

"Now it's your turn," I said.

Nancy quickly started undressing and Jen followed after a moment's hesitation. Soon they were both naked so I kicked off my jeans. No one touched but I walked around them and took a good look. Both had full, dark bushes. Nancy was sprouting what would eventually be a nice set of tits. I felt a little awkward because one of them was my sister but I quickly got over that. I asked Nancy if she wanted to touch my dick but she declined. After a couple of minutes everyone got dressed and the girls went upstairs to Jen's room, probably for a debriefing. I went to my room and jerked off.

Later that afternoon I was in the kitchen. My parents were home now and dinner was just about ready. The girls came down from my sister's room, Nancy was leaving. As she was heading out the door Nancy walked close by and said softly, "I wanted to." Then she left. I had to think about what she meant. Did she mean she wanted to do what they did? Or did she want to touch it? I would ponder that question when I went to bed later that night as I jerked off for the third time that day.

My sister was reluctant to talk about what happened so I couldn't find out from her what Nancy meant. I figured I would have to wait until I could somehow talk to Nancy. It turned put I didn't have to wait long at all. Two days later I had just gotten home and had the house to myself for a couple of hours. This was my favorite day of the week because I could masturbate without having to worry about someone walking in on me. I barely got settled when the door bell rang. I reluctantly went to answer it.

I opened the door and it was Nancy. "Jen's not here, she has band practice today."

"I know. I was….I was hoping I could see it again and…maybe touch it."

Without a word I ushered her in and we went to my room. I could tell she was really nervous so I talked a bit to get her to relax. I was going to tell her to get undressed but didn't want to chance scaring her away. I had her sit on the bed and I stood in front of her and took my pants off. I stood directly in front of her with my very erect cock.

"Go ahead, touch it."

Her fingertips traced the head and then the shaft.

"It looks so hard but the skin feels so soft."

"You can rub it."

She did lightly.

"Wrap your fingers around it and rub."

Her fingers circle my dick and she slid her hand up and down a bit. It was time to go for more.

"Take your clothes off, I want to see you."

"Just my top."

She removed her shirt and bra without getting up.

"You took it all off the other day."

"I know, maybe next time."

Next time? Okay, I could deal with that. It was time to see how far I could go with her this time.

She let me touch her tits and I sucked on her nipples for a little while. After a few minutes a leaned back, took her hand, and put it on my cock.

"Rub it some more, make me cum."

"What do you mean?"

"Make it…you don't know?"

She looked puzzled. "Know what?"

"That stuff shoots out."

"What stuff?"

"You don't know," I shook my head. "It's called cumming and it feels really good. You rub it and white stuff will shoot out. Just do it and you'll see, but don't stop rubbing until I tell you, ok?"

"Ok"

She started stroking and I could feel myself getting ready to explode.

"That's it…a little faster…that's it. Oh, that feels good. Get ready…here it comes."

Ughh!

I shot a stream into the air and she gasped in surprise.

"Keep going."

She kept pumping until I was empty and put my hand on hers to stop her.

"That was so cool!" She rubbed her fingers in my semen. "It's all gooey and sticky."

"Do you ever touch yourself down there?" I asked.

"Sometimes a little, it feels funny."

"Well if you keep doing it you'll cum and feel good too, you'll get wet but stuff won't shoot out."

"I'll have to try."

"Take your pants off and I'll rub it."

"Next time," she said. "It's yucky down there right now."

"Oh, I get it. No problem."

I took a washcloth I kept in my nightstand and started cleaning up. She took the cloth from me and wiped up the goo. She also fondled my balls a little. Then she put her bra and shirt back on and said she had to leave.

"That was fun," she said. "I like playing with it. Can I do it again?"

"Anytime."

"Next week? But don't tell Jen."

"Don't worry, I wasn't planning to."

Power Shift

Brad was drinking at the local bar, typical for a Friday. Actually typical for any day that ends in 'y.' He was in a foul mood; the cause was a rumor about his sister and it wasn't good. He wasn't so concerned about her; he feared it would make him look bad. He'd overhead a couple of guys talking about the girl with the big tits that worked at the corner convenience store – that would be his younger sister. While he was used to guys making comments about her because she was pretty hot, it was what they said that bothered him. He didn't want to believe it but he suspected it was true. It would certainly explain a lot.

Jessica seemed to have a lot of cash lately, certainly more than she could make at her job. He thought about confronting her but she would just deny it. He needed proof. Thinking about what to do next, he ordered a shot from the barmaid, not that he needed it since he was pretty drunk. It did give him the courage he required to see if what he'd heard was right. He left a tip on the bar and walked out the door. The sudden blast of cold air momentarily sobered him as he walked to his car. He drove across town and pulled into the parking lot of the *Tender Trap Gentleman's Club*.

He paid the cover and walked inside. He scanned the place as his eyes adjusted; no sign of his sister. He hoped the guys were wrong. He found a spot in the corner where he would not easily be seen. He watched as dancers stripped, after three had performed he'd had enough. They were not very exciting and nothing much to look at. The third one left the stage and he was about to leave but felt something in the crowd, it seemed to be a heightened sense of anticipation. He watched as the next dancer came out and the sparse crowd started howling with delight. He was transfixed – it was his sister.

She was four years younger than him, having just turned eighteen, and he couldn't believe what he was seeing. For several years now, ever since she reached puberty and sprouted a massive set of mammaries, he'd been trying to get a peek at her naked. Now he was about to get a show but he wasn't happy about it. He watched transfixed as she stripped. She wasn't very good but it didn't matter to the guys watching her. He understood why, she was impressively put together, what his grandfather used to call 'a burlap bag full of bobcat.' When she'd stripped to her g-string he realized he had a massive erection. He knew he should feel guilty or ashamed, but he didn't. After all, he had tried spying on her and even used her panties to jerk off. Besides, he told himself, it's not like he wanted to fuck her, he only wanted to see her naked.

By the time she left the stage she had collected plenty of tips, flirting with the customers as she sauntered off. He left and went home, wondering what to do next. It was really none of his business. Brad wasn't thinking about his sister's honor or anything quite so moral. He was wondering how he could use this information to his advantage. If their parents found out what she was doing they would be devastated, especially if their friends at church found out. They'd probably throw Jessica out of the house, if not outright disown her. They'd rather lose a daughter than tarnish their reputation. Having a son who was a drunk was bad enough, having a daughter who stripped, and who knew what else, would be more than they could bear.

When he got home Brad went into the house as quietly as he could, his parents were asleep. He thought about his sister and realized he still had an erection. He slipped into her room and took a pair of panties out of her drawer, then went back to his room. He took off his clothes and got into bed. Wrapping Jessica's panties around his dick, he jerked off.

Several days later he was alone in the house. His parents had gone to a religious retreat for the weekend. Jessica came home with several packages from the mall and dropped them in her room. He quietly walked to her door and saw her taking several expensive looking outfits out of the bags.

"Whoa, that's nice stuff," he said.

She smiled at him, "You like it?"

"Yeah, though I didn't realize 7-Eleven paid so well."

He watched her face and noticed a hint of worry. "I…I've been saving my money."

"Or maybe getting some big tips."

She tried to laugh, "I don't get tips at the store."

"I wasn't referring to the store."

Her face flushed. "What…what are you talking about?"

"I know what you're doing."

"I'm not doing anything."

He laughed. "You're stripping at the *Trap*, I saw you."

She didn't say anything; she just hung her new clothes up in the closet.

"What do you think will happen if mom and dad find out?"

Her face was aghast, as if she hadn't considered the possibility. "They won't find out."

"They will if someone they know sees you," he said, "or if I tell them."

She stared at him in anger. "You wouldn't tell them."

"Depends," he said. "What's in it for me?"

"What? I have to pay you?"

He leered at her. "Oh, I don't want your money?"

"Wha…what do you want?"

He smiled at her, "Strip!"

"What? I'm not gonna…"

"You do it for strangers; you can do it for me. Take your clothes off….and make it sexy."

"I'm not…"

"Strip!"

He walked into the room and sat on her bed. He reached over to her nightstand and turned on the music. "Do it."

A look of humiliation on her face, she began slowly removing her clothes.

The following Friday night Jessica was in the dressing room of the club getting ready for her turn on the stage. She had been at this for a month now and it was getting more difficult to do her regular job. She made more in four hours stripping than she did all week at the convenience store, but she had to keep that job as cover.

The dressing room was in a constant state of controlled chaos with girls were coming in and out as they went to perform or returned after they finished up. She liked the girls she worked with and everyone seemed to get along. As the dancers sat around chatting while in various states of undress she joined the conversation. She started with idle chatter but was itching to share what had happened with her brother. Though she stripped for him, she refused to take off her g-string by maintaining she never took it off when she danced. He tried to insist she remove it but she wouldn't; that was her line in the sand. Still, she couldn't get over the humiliation, it was her *brother*!

"I was so humiliated last week," she said to the girl sitting next to her. "My brother found out I was dancing here."

"Could be worse," she responded while looking in the mirror and applying makeup. "We had a girl here last year, her name was Maddie; her dad came into the club and caught her. We never saw her after that."

"Wow, that sucks. My parents would disown me – or worse. That's the problem, my brother used that to blackmail me and make me strip for him."

"That's no big deal, my brother sees me naked all the time. By the way, I'm Candie."

"Jessica. My family is ultra religious, no nudity allowed. That's why it was so humiliating."

The girl on the other side of her, Robin, chimed in. "The same thing happened to me. You have to turn it to your advantage."

"How?" Jessica asked.

"Right now he has the power, you have to take it back. You need to have something to hold over him that's worse than what he has over you."

"But what? I don't have anything. What could be worse?"

Robin asked, "Is he older or younger?"

"Older."

"Perfect. Was he turned on when you stripped?"

Jessica laughed. "By the bulge in his pants I'd say so."

Canide giggled. "When you see the bulge, go for the tips!"

"So true," Robin said. "That bulge tells you he wants more than to just see you naked."

Jessica was aghast. "You're…you're not suggesting I fuck my brother."

"No need to go that far. Besides making me show him my tits my brother wanted to touch them. The first time he just looked, the second time he touched, the third time he sucked my nipples. It was the fourth time that changed the power dynamic."

"What happened?"

"I knew it would keep getting worse," Robin said. "So I took matters into my own hand – literally."

"What do you mean?"

"The next time he tried it I 'accidentally' touched his dick through his pants. On cue, he took it out and told me to touch it. I played hard to get."

"Was it big?" Candie asked.

"Not at all." Robin continued, "He grabbed my hand and made me touch it. I pretended to resist but I eventually did. I wound up giving him a hand job…lasted all of thirty seconds. Since then I've owned him, the power was all mine."

"How so?"

"He's older, like your brother, so I told him if he said anything I'd say he was molesting me. That last time I recorded it so I had evidence."

"That sounds devious," Jessica said.

"No more devious than him making me show my tits."

"I guess," Jessica said. "And he never bothered you after that?"

Robin laughed. "I still let him see me sometimes, but he's my puppy dog. Whenever I want something I get it by showing my boobs, but it's always on my terms."

"That girl Maddie used to fuck her brother," Candie said.

"True," Robin replied. "But she wanted to."

Brad knew he should feel guilty about what he made his sister do, but he didn't. It was just another one of his character flaws. It was obvious that the dynamic of their relationship had changed; no surprise there. She was pissed at him for sure, but that's what she gets for being a stripper. She certainly had the body for it. He knew she was hot but seeing her naked was surreal; he wished she had taken her g-string off. He'll get her to do that next time and there would be a next time.

The next Sunday, while her parents were in church, Brad walked into her room while she was lounging in bed watching TV. He made small talk but she knew what he wanted. She also suspected him of something and decided to confront him if he asked her to strip again. Based on the way he was looking at her she figured he was about to do just that.

"I guess you danced the other night."

"I did."

"So do it for me, take your clothes off."

"I did that already."

"You danced again, so strip again. That's your payment for me to keep quiet."

"Fuck you."

"Do it!"

Fuming, she threw back the cover and stood in front of him. She was only wearing a nightshirt and panties. She pulled it over her head and tossed it aside, standing there in her underwear. He smiled at her as she watched the bulge in his pants grow. He motioned for her to turn around so she did.

"Take the panties off."

"I told you before, I'm not doing that."

"C'mon."

"No. Speaking of panties, what are you doing with them?"

"I don't know what you're talking about."

She decided to bluff. "I know you're stealing them."

"I'm not…"

"Don't lie to me. Tell me and I'll take them off."

His hesitation told her she was right. She was missing at least four pair, including her favorite. She stood semi-naked looking at him with her hands on her hips. She could feel the power shifting her way just like Robin said.

"I'm waiting."

Brad whispered, "Rub myself."

"I didn't hear that, what?"

"I said I rub myself."

Jessica knew what he meant but acted confused. "Rub yourself? How?"

"I rub them on my dick, ok?"

She smiled in triumph. She peeled off her underwear and tossed it at him. He caught them as his eyes locked in on the landing strip of hair just above the flowering protrusion of her labia.

"Show me."

Brad held her panties wearing a look of confusion. "What?"

"Show me how you do it?"

"You…you want me to show you?"

"Yes. What's the matter, are you shy?"

As she stood there, now stark naked, she watched him fumble with his belt. He slowly took out his erect cock. She had to work to maintain her stoic expression, his dick was impressive. He wrapped her panties around his penis and tugged a few times. He stopped, unraveled them, and looked up at her.

"I don't think you're done," she said.

"You…you want me to keep…"

She looked down at him, hands on her hips, "Yes."

"But I'll…."

"Cum? Isn't that what happens when you use them?"

"Yes"

"Then you better keep going."

He wrapped the panties around again and resumed jerking his cock. She stared at him as he fixed his eyes on her crotch and stroked faster. She saw his eyes close as he started breathing heavier. He grunted as a stream of semen shot in the air followed by several shorter spurts. He ejaculated all over himself, her bed and the floor; it was quite a load. As he was catching his breath she picked up her nightshirt and slipped it on. She grabbed the panties out of his hand as she walked toward the door.

"Now clean up your fuckin' mess; I better not see one drop of your goo anywhere. And I want my panties back, all of them!"

She left the room and walked down the hall smiling. She could feel the dynamic change, the power was beginning to shift

Several days later she walked into her room and saw something on top of her dresser. She walked over and smiled. There were not four, but six pair of panties. All had been washed and neatly folded. She cheerfully put them in her drawer. The power is all mine big brother!

The following Sunday, like clockwork, Brad came into her bedroom while she was watching TV. She danced her usual Friday night shift and assumed he would be looking for his "payment." It was like a mafia payoff for "Protection," except she wasn't having it. The power was all hers now; at least she thought it was. She would soon find out.

"You danced again Friday," he said.

"You know I did."

"Time to pay up; show me something."

"Not happening. You've seen me twice, that's enough. If you want to see more you'll have to come to the club."

"Look, you strip or I'll spill the beans and you're done."

"No you won't."

She saw him hesitate, the look of confidence gone. She was nervous but did her best not to show it, his uncertainty was obvious.

"I wouldn't be so sure," he said in a shaky voice.

She looked up at him with a smile. "Oh, but I am."

"How can you be so confident?"

"If you tell mom and dad," she said, "I'll tell them that you forced me to strip and used my panties to masturbate."

"They'll never believe you."

She didn't say a word. She retrieved something from her nightstand. It was a voice-activated tape recorder she had discretely placed on top of her dresser the previous week. She pushed play and watched the blood drain from his face and he clearly heard himself telling her to strip followed by the discussion of his stealing her underwear. That, of course, was followed by the sound of his grunt when he ejaculated.

"You…you wouldn't play that."

She grinned again. "Sure about that?"

"But it implicates you too, we'll both be ruined."

"True," she said. "It's MAD."

"It's nuts alright."

"No, MAD – Mutually Assured Destruction," she said. "If you take me down you're going with me. But if they throw me out I can obviously support myself, can you? And in case you were wondering, I have a copy of the tape."

"Let's not be hasty. I didn't mean anything by it. It's just….it's just that you are so hot and, well I don't exactly have chicks, hot or otherwise, throwing themselves at me."

Her attitude softened and her eyes moistened. She suddenly saw him as incredibly vulnerable and she felt bad for him.

She smiled. "You think I'm hot?"

"That ass and those jugs? Damn straight I do; not to mention, you're gorgeous."

She knew he meant it and a tear slowly rolled down her cheek.

"That is so sweet. Why can't you always talk to me like that?"

"Because I'm an asshole."

"Well, I won't argue with you there, but you don't have to be."

"If I hadn't been would you have showed me your tits?"

"You're not being an asshole now." With that she pulled her shirt over her head and sat there topless. She saw his eyes go wide and glanced to his crotch to see the telltale bulge quickly form.

"By the way, you have a nice dick."

"Really," she said. "Show it to be again, but don't get any ideas; I just want to look."

He dropped his pants and stood proudly as his he moved from side to side showing her his erection. It really was a nice cock; long, thick, with a very nice mushroom head. If he wasn't her brother she'd be all over it.

"Okay, put it away," she said. "Maybe we can come to a truce. I'll let you see me naked sometimes as long as you're not a pig about it."

He had a big smile on his face. "Deal!"

She got up out of the bed and went to her dresser. She opened the drawer and took out a pair of panties, one of her least favorites, and tossed them to him.

"You better go take care of that thing before it explodes. And I want them back and they better be clean."

"Yes ma'am!" He left the room smiling and clutching his treasure as he went to take care of business.

She smiled and whispered, "Oh yeah, the power is all mine!"

Punishment Glory

Daddy is not my real dad; I just call him that because he takes care of me. I don't mean to break Daddy's rules, but I make mistakes sometimes. Okay, lots of times. Today I was really bad, and daddy was so angry. He made me take a time out in the dark room, really just an empty closet with a chair, while he thought about what to do to me. I hoped it wasn't going to be the switch again; that hurt so much last time.

Finally the door opened and Daddy waited for me to come out. I knelt in front of him with my head down, eyes locked on his boots.

"What am I going to do with you, Princess?"

I like when he calls me "Princess," that means he can't be *that* mad.

"Punish me Daddy, I was so bad."

"I know Princess, but the usual punishment doesn't seem to work. We're going to have to try something different."

The way he said that scared me, I even peed myself a little. What was he going to do that was worse than beating me with the switch? I kept looking at his boots, not daring to move.

"Get up Princess, we're going for a ride."

"Whe…where are we going?"

Daddy didn't answer; he just led me outside to the car. I went to get in the passenger but he told me to get in the back. After I was buckled in put a blindfold on me and told me not to even think about removing it. The car started and we drove for about twenty minutes. I felt the car go over a bump as if we entered a parking lot. The car came to a stop and the engine turned off. I didn't dare move.

"Let's go Princess, keep the blindfold on."

Daddy led me along. We went through a door and then across a wooden floor. We stopped for a moment; Daddy seemed to be opening a door. A few seconds later we were through it and Daddy helped me sit on a stool. He took the blindfold off. I was in a dark box of a room with walls painted black. It was a larger version of my punishment room at home. Daddy lifted a flap on the wall revealing a narrow slit.

"This is your punishment, Princess. You're in a glory hole."

"This is my punishment?"

"Yes Princess. You're going to suck every cock that comes through that hole. You're a good little cock sucker, aren't you, Princess?"

"Yes Daddy, I'm a very good cock sucker."

"Good. You're to suck everyone until they cum. Then you're to swallow every drop. If any gets on the floor or walls you're to lick it up. Do you understand Princess?"

"Yes Daddy."

"Who's a dirty, slut, whore?"

"I am Daddy!"

"Any questions, Princess?"

"How will I know when I'm done, Daddy?"

"My cock will be the last one. Now get to work.

"Yes Daddy!"

I couldn't believe that this was my punishment. I love sucking cock, especially Daddy's. A lot of times Daddy makes me suck his friends' cocks, but his is the absolute best.

I heard footsteps and a few seconds later a penis came through the opening. It wasn't a very big one and I immediately started sucking on it and licking it. It only took about a minute before it exploded in my mouth. I swallowed every drop and made sure none dripped on the floor. I wished it wasn't so quick but Daddy's friends say they cum really fast when I suck them because I'm so good at it.

The next one came in right away. This one was much bigger and didn't cum as fast. I was able to really enjoy myself for a while. I worked it for three or four minutes before it shot a load down my throat.

By now my eyes had adjusted to the light so I could get a good look at the beautiful cocks. The next one that came in was so pretty, almost as nice as Daddy's. I wanted to really take my time and savor it. This one ejaculated in a couple of minutes and I was disappointed to see it go.

The next one came almost as soon as I put it in my mouth, but the one after lasted at least ten minutes. By the time I was done with that one my mouth was feeling sore. Fortunately the one after that exploded really fast.

The next one that came in made me happy and sad. Happy because it was Daddy, but sad because it meant I was done. I wanted to go really slow. Sometimes I can suck on Daddy for almost an hour before he cums because I know his triggers and how to slow them down. But Daddy must have been in a hurry because he started humping my mouth and came in about a minute.

I sat back on my chair hoping I might get another one but instead the door opened and daddy was standing there. He had a flashlight and shined the beam on the walls and floor.

"You didn't spill a drop. Good work, Princess."

"Thank you, Daddy."

We went back to the car and started driving home.

"Daddy?"

"Yes, Princess?"

"You know I love to suck cock, right Daddy?"

"Of course."

"Then how was that a punishment? It was more like a reward."

Daddy got that evil grin that scares me. I was afraid of what he was going to say.

"How many men do you work with, Princess?"

"Counting bosses?"

"Yes, Princess."

I thought for a moment. "Twelve"

"That's right, Princess. Not counting mine, how many cocks did you suck today?"

I thought for a moment before proudly saying, "Six."

"That's right Princess. Those six are all guys you work with. Now when you go to your job and look around at all the guys you won't know which ones you sucked off and which you didn't."

I sat quietly for a minute before asking, "Do they know it was me?"

"Oh yes, Princess. Now they know what a dirty little, cock sucking whore you are."

I sat there brooding, thinking about what this would mean at work. I tried to think of a way to keep this from becoming a disaster. After about ten minutes I had an idea.

"Daddy?"

"Yes, Princess?"

"Can I blow the rest of them?"

Mommy Too Dearest

The office décor highlighted an obvious effort for cheerfulness, no doubt an attempt to comfort the visitors who most likely felt far from jovial. She scanned the flowers on the table, surprisingly real, the Monet reproductions on the wall, the assorted knickknacks, and the soothing paint colors. It did not make her any less apprehensive. She still didn't understand why she was here. She did appreciate her shrink's integrity in sending her; certainly better than the first creep she consulted.

Sure, her issued involved sex, but the problem was certainly mental not physical. When that first jerk insisted he had to examine "the inner workings of her sexuality," aka her tits and pussy, she told him to "fuck off," literally, and stormed out. Her initial instinct was to scrap the notion of seeking help but knew she had to give it another try. The second psychiatrist, Dr. Richardson, was much better and put her at ease with his professionalism. She explained her issue but just when she was feeling comfortable and that she'd made the right choice, he suggested she see someone else. He felt her issue was rooted in her sexuality but did not feel he was the best one to help her. He highly recommended a psychologist who specialized in sexual issues.

Now she sat in the waiting room of Dr. Glenda Plotke, PsyD, CST. She had convinced herself it was not a sexual issue but here she sat, at her shrink's recommendation, in the office of a clinical psychologist who dealt primarily in sex related problems. On the one hand it was easier to discuss such things with a woman, on the other the issue was such a societal taboo that she would expect another woman to find her repulsive. Dr. Richardson assured her that would not be the case but she wasn't so sure. He was a man after all, and most men would probably find her problem titillating. Her heart sank and she felt a lump in her throat when the door opened and her name was called.

She had been worried that the therapist might be a much older person, a grandmotherly type, which would make it difficult to open up. She was relieved when Dr. Plotke turned out to be in her early fifties, only a little older than her. The initial discussion was little more than information gathering and a very general discussion about her sexual history and her divorce that happened three years earlier. The therapist had an easy manner about her and she was immediately comfortable. That is, until she wasn't.

"So tell me why you're here," the therapist began.

"Didn't Doctor Richardson tell you?"

"He told me in very general terms that you had an issue that was more suited to my area of expertise. He didn't go into specifics because he did not want me to prejudge anything."

"Well, Doctor Plotke…"

"Call me Glenda."

"Glenda," she started, "I have a problem with my son."

"How old is he?"

"Nineteen, he still lives with me."

"Tell me about your issue."

She felt a lump in her throat and her heart was beating so fast she expected it to jump out of her chest. She rubbed her suddenly sweaty palms together and tried to gather herself.

"I…I want….I want to fuck him."

There, she said it. Out loud. A secret she had never verbalized to anyone. There was an overwhelming sense of catharsis which was quickly replaced by dread. Would the doctor think she was some sort of monster?

Glenda looked at her without any visible reaction. "When did you first feel this way?"

"It was a couple of years ago, though it wasn't so much about having sex."

"Tell me what you remember."

"It was about a year after my divorce."

She told the story in great detail because she remembered it so clearly. It was wash day and she had retrieved the basket of dirty laundry from her son's room like she always did. As she was putting his briefs into the washing machine she noticed a dry, whitish stain and smiled. He was jerking off. As she was putting the rest of the clothes into the machine she noticed another pair had evidence of masturbation – and it was still wet. It was fresh, probably only minutes old. She confirmed this by rubbing it between her fingers and them licking them. *She has just tasted her son's semen.* She felt a tingling in her crotch and could feel herself getting wet. She finished loading the washing machine, added detergent and started the cycle. She went to her room, locked the door and turned on the television to hide the sound. She quickly stripped off her jeans and underwear, plopped down on the bed, retrieved her toy from the nightstand and vibrated herself to a massive orgasm.

"But your son was never involved in any way?" Glenda asked.

"No, Jerry, my son was not. But I *tasted* his semen! I would never do that with my husband; it was one of the things he hated about me. I would give him oral but I wouldn't swallow. I wouldn't even let him do it in my mouth."

Glenda wrote something in her notebook. "Were there any other incidents after that?"

"I'll say. I became obsessed. Not right away, but over time; it was a progressive thing."

She told her how she kept trying to see Jerry naked; she also tried to let him see her nude. She was proud of her body and worked hard to keep it in shape. Her large breasts, mega-tits her husband called them, had always turned heads. Her nipples were dark, round, and the perfect size she thought. Her pussy, she was often told, was quite tasty and she kept her pubes neatly trimmed but refused to go along with the trend to shave it. She felt a nice, dark bush added an air of mystery to an otherwise plain area. She was sure Jerry caught a few glimpses of her naked when she purposely left her door partly open while he was home. She hadn't seen him though, but she was would change that.

His bathroom was the Jack-and-Jill variety that connected his room to the extra bedroom. The guest bedroom side was always kept closed and locked. She disabled the lock and left the door slightly ajar.

She assumed he wouldn't check since the guest room was never occupied. If the door from his room to the bathroom was open she would be able to have a direct view to his bed. If his light was on she would be able to see clearly. She placed some boxes of clothes in the guest room so she would have a plausible reason to be in there.

Over the next several days she slipped into the guest room when her son went into his. She didn't see anything much. He would sit on his bed and watch TV, do homework, or read. He changed a few times but it was always out of her line of sight. She only stayed a few minutes each time since she was afraid of being caught. She felt guilty about doing this but she could not stop herself. It was in the second week when something finally happened. She was about to leave the guestroom when she saw a flash of skin. He came back into view facing away from her. She gasped audibly and hoped he didn't hear, though his TV was on loud enough to mask the sound. His ass was perfect, though that can be expected from an athletic boy of seventeen. Her heart skipped a beat when he turned around and started walking into the bathroom. She quickly slipped out of the room but what she had seen was etched into her brain. The dangling penis, it was big, the testicles hanging below a patch of dark pubic hair. Back in her own room on her bed, her eyes were closed as she masturbated while imagining what he must look like erect.

She wouldn't have to wait long. The next night he went to his room earlier than usual; he normally stayed with her watching TV after dinner. When she was sure he wasn't coming back she quietly slipped into the guest room. She settled in and could tell he was walking around the room but didn't see him. She heard his dresser draw open and shut and seconds later he was in her line of sight. He was naked and holding something in his hand, it was a magazine. As he turned she saw it – he was erect.

To her it was massive, seven or more inches and it was standing straight up as only young boys do. He sat on the bed and flipped through the pages of the magazine. Her eyes were glued to his cock. After a few seconds of rifling through the magazine's pages he seemed to settle on one and placed it flat on his bed. He then turned on his side, facing toward her, and began to slowly stroke his cock while his eyes were on the magazine. Her own hand slipped inside the sweats she was wearing and she masturbated along with him. He started pumping fast and his head dropped, his eyes closed. She bit into the fabric of her top to stifle the sound of her own orgasm that occurred seconds after he exploded in what seemed like an endless stream. As she recovered her senses she saw his hand drop away from his cock as it deflated. As he cleaned up the large puddle of goo, she collected herself and slipped out of the room.

"What kind of creep watches her own son masturbate? I mean, my god, I got off watching him jerk off. What's wrong with me?"

"Don't be so hard on yourself," Glenda said. "You hadn't had sex since your divorce and had a lot of pent up sexual energy. Was it just that one time?"

She laughed. "One time? That was just the start of it. I watched him dozens of times."

Glenda started writing again. "Tell me more."

She told Glenda about understanding her son's habits and patterns. She soon came to know when he was going to masturbate. Though she was sometimes thwarted by a closed door or a darkened room, she usually had a good view. The problem was that this soon wasn't enough. Though overwhelmed with guilt, she imagined her hand replacing his. She wondered what he felt like; she imagined the throbbing and pulsating of his cock as he ejaculated. It was Jerry who inspired her to take it up a notch, though he did so innocently.

She was always touchy-feely with him and had been since he was a baby. If he was sitting at the kitchen table she would run her hand across his broad, muscular shoulders as she passed. One day while talking to him she stood behind him and massaged his shoulders. Though she sometimes did so, this time she spent a little more time and kneaded his muscles a bit more intensely.

He moaned slightly. "Mmm. Mom, you've got great hands; you should do that professionally."

She smiled as she kept rubbing. "That's a great idea; I'll have to think about that."

While she had no intention of changing careers, she did think about what he said. She remembered a brochure for adult education classes at the community college and hoped she hadn't thrown it away. She hadn't, and she found what she was looking for. There was a class offered for beginning massage that began a couple of weeks later and she promptly signed herself up.

She looked up at Glenda. "I signed up to get my hands on my son; what was I thinking? I even bought a massage table for the house."

"And you used it?"

"Not right away. Jerry was happy I was taking the class; he thought I needed to get out more. He let me practice on him but I only did chair massages of his back and shoulders. He didn't know I had the table at first."

Glenda scribbled on her pad. "So this is when things escalated?"

"Yes"

After several weeks of practicing chair massages she decided it was time. She set the table up in the corner of the living room. When Jerry saw this he asked her what this was about and she explained she was up to full body massages and needed to practice.

Jerry asked, "Who are you going to practice on?"

"You, hop on."

He hesitated a moment before sitting on the table.

"I can't massage you with your clothes on."

"I…I have to get undressed?"

"Leave your underwear on if you want, or put on a swimsuit if you're shy."

"It's not that I'm shy, it just seems weird."

He left the room and came back wearing his swim trunks. He was face down on the table to start. She worked slowly, focusing on each muscle group. He seemed a little uncomfortable when she got down to his thighs but soon relaxed. She was careful to avoid his private parts; she wanted to gain his trust. This continued two or three times a week for several weeks and he was not only relaxed, he looked forward to the sessions. She noticed he was getting erections during the massages so she was looking to take things a little further.

When he came out for the next session she was holding a small towel. He looked at her quizzically.

"I need you to take everything off today, I have to practice buttocks massage. You can cover yourself with this."

"You're…you're going to massage my butt?"

"Yes, don't be such a prude; the gluteus maximus is a muscle and it's part of massage therapy."

She worked the full massage, including his glutes. When he turned on his back he was very careful to keep the towel positioned to hide his crotch. She worked from head to toe and back up. As she worked on his inner thigh his erection popped up right on cue. *It was so close.* She wanted to grab it but resisted. She finished the massage and let him off the table.

"Glenda, I was such a schemer; I don't understand what was going through my head."

"But you resisted the temptation," Glenda said.

"That time."

They were at it again a few days later. While he was face down and she was working his inner thigh near his ass she 'slipped' and touched his scrotum for an instant. She would have expected him to flinch but he didn't even react. When he rolled over on his back he was already erect, that usually didn't happen until later. As she worked his neck and chest her eyes were fixed on the bulge in the towel. She saw it throb a few times. *He must be really horny today.* She decided to comment.

"Looks like someone's enjoying the massage today." She arched her eyebrows and nodded toward his crotch.

"Mom!"

"Oh relax, it's normal."

"But…"

She reached down, grabbed the towel, and flung it off exposing his cock. He looked at her in shock but it wasn't going down. He also made no effort to cover up and just let her keep massaging his chest.

"But I…but.."

"You're uncomfortable being naked in front of your mother?"

"A little."

She shook her head. "People are so hung up on nudity, it's so stupid. You know the penis is just a muscle. In a proper massage it gets taken care of too.

"But you're…"

Without another word she moved to the middle of the table, poured some oil in her hand, and rubbed it on his cock. The other hand kneaded his testicles. In a matter of seconds he was moaning and breathing heavy. The semen shot two feet in the air as he quickly ejaculated. She kept stroking until he was empty. She grabbed a damp towel from the side table and wiped up the mess. Then she resumed the massage as if nothing happened.

"I jerked off my own son. It's not something that just happened; I plotted this for months and pulled it off – literally."

Glenda looked up from her pad. "Did you want him to touch you?"

"No, I really just wanted to make him comfortable. My fantasies were always about me playing with his dick, I never thought about him touching me."

"But things didn't stop there."

"No"

Jerry was acting awkward, which didn't surprise her. She felt guilty about what she had done but, strangely, she did not regret it. She also wanted to do it again. For that to happen she would have to put his mind at ease.

"It was just a massage," she told him.

"But you…you…"

"Made you ejaculate?"

"Well…"

"And you enjoyed it, no?"

"But…"

"Yes or no?"

"Yes"

"So what's the problem? It's not like we had sex, I gave you a massage – a complete one."

"I know but…"

"Look, if you don't want me to do that I won't next time."

"No it's..."

"No, what? Do you want me to do that next time or not?"

"Yes"

"Fine. Then don't be hung up about it. I know it made you a little uncomfortable, maybe I shouldn't have done it. Do you me to stop giving you massages?"

"No"

She smiled. "Now we're getting somewhere. Take your pants off and get on the table."

He didn't hesitate and slipped his jeans and briefs off. He laid back, his shirt still on. She poured the oil in her hand and slowly stroked him. He didn't seem ready to explode so she was able to take her time.

She looked up at Glenda expecting to see a look of disgust, but her expression was neutral, as if she heard this every day.

"I assume this is still going on," Glenda said.

"Two, three times a week."

"And you're feeling guilty about it."

"That's just it – I don't. But now I want to fuck him. I know it's wrong but I don't feel guilty about that either. What's wrong with me?"

Glenda took a few more notes. "When is the last time you actually had sex?"

She didn't have to think very hard. "I haven't gotten laid since my husband left."

Glenda nodded knowingly. "Why do *you* think you really want to fuck your son?"

"Because he's safe….I don't have to risk being rejected?"

"Ding-ding-ding….we have a winner!"

"So…so what do I do?"

Glenda opened her appointment book. "Come back one week from today."

"Okay and then?"

Glenda smiled. "You can tell me all about the guy you had sex with between now and then…and it better not be your son."

Not So Blind Date

I am nervous, more nervous than anticipating a blind date. At least on a blind date you know going in that there's a good possibility that it won't work out. You might not like her, she might not like you, there's no attraction, no spark; any number of things could go wrong. If you liked her but she didn't like you, well that's how it goes sometimes. You get over it, you move on. But this is different.

I've already met her. She is attractive and she is, shall we say, well-assembled. Nice boobs, great ass, and in great shape. A strong, but not overpowering, personality and she seems like a lot of fun. She also has my favorite quality – enthusiasm. She claims to really enjoy sex and I have absolutely no reason to doubt that. To top it off she gives unbelievably good hugs and I would love to cuddle with her. I really like her.

So why am I so nervous? Simply put, I am afraid I might not measure up. Not in that sense, if she takes a ruler to me I'll be just fine. You see, I haven't had intercourse in five years. My sex life consists of the occasional half-assed blow job and a whole lot of jerking off. Of course I'm getting ahead of myself; I have no idea if she even wants to fuck me. I hope she does but I'd settle for another hug at this point. I'd be in heaven if she let me eat her, I have a feeling she tastes absolutely delicious.

Well, here I am at her house. I was surprised she suggested I pick her up rather than meet somewhere. When I asked what she would like to do, she said we should just play it by ear. That was fine by me as long as it included a hug. I went to her front door and rang the bell. She opens it in a matter of seconds and smiles at me while inviting me inside. She is wearing blue jeans and a t-shirt and looked casual and relaxed. That's fine, I am nervous enough for both of us.

"Would you like water, beer, a soda?"

"A beer would be great."

A little alcohol should help with the nerves. I had thought about jerking off before coming over to lessen the anxiety but quickly realized it wouldn't help. But her easy manner is contagious and I am starting to relax. She gives me a beer and has one herself as we sit next to each other on her sofa. Her living room is pretty sparse, just a coffee table, TV, sofa and end table, and a picture on the wall of a pastoral scene. The center of the room is just a big empty space.

She is so easy to talk to. She tells me more about her, I share things about me. I am content to just spend the day here without going out at all. I am just about at the end of my beer when she chugs down the last few ounces of hers. She puts the bottle down on the table, shifts a little to face me and smiles.

"It's time to get to know each other better."

"I thought that's what we were doing," I say.

"Well yeah, but let's take it up a notch. Go stand over there, in the middle of the room."

I hesitate a moment, then get up. "Here?"

"That's good," she says. "Now take your shirt off."

She looks at me with a bemused expression and arches her eyebrows as if to say "let's go already." I pull my shirt over my head and toss it on a chair. She just stares at me without a word.

"Good, now the pants."

"Huh?"

"Take your pants off, the underwear too."

"What? Why?"

"C'mon, just do it already."

She arches her eyebrows again. Feeling embarrassed, I turn my back to her, kick off my shoes and step out of my pants, tossing them with the shirt. I pull the briefs off and toss them too. I am stark naked. I feel myself blushing as I turn around to face her – my cock is hard as a rock.

She just sits there, fully dressed, not making a move or a sound. She is just looking at me as I stand there. After a couple of minutes she gets up and walks toward me and circles around where I stand. I feel as if I am being inspected. She brushes her fingers on my butt cheeks and comes around in front of me – I am still at attention.

She squats down so her eyes are at cock level. She doesn't touch, just looks. She brings her hands up to cup my balls which are now very tight, a combination of being a little cold and ready to explode. Fortunately she lets go before I do. Then she goes back to the sofa and sits down but keeps looking at me. Isn't she going to get undressed?

"Okay," she says. "It's time for the cuddle test. Come over here."

I walk back to the sofa and she scoots over so I can sit down. Then she wraps herself around me as she curls her feet up on the couch. I am very tense but trying to relax. This is a first for me; I have never been totally naked while cuddling a fully-clothed woman. Her head is on my chest and her fingers caress my stomach, they go past my cock without making contact, and then stroke my thighs. I am ready to explode and haven't even been touched. But I relax. My erection actually starts to subside a bit, which is a relief. Then she brings her mouth to mine and we kiss. Her lips part as her tongue probes my mouth, and then mine hers. My erection is back with a vengeance. After a few minutes she gets up and leaves the room.

She returns moments later wearing a white, terrycloth robe. Her legs are bare so I know she'd gotten undressed. She comes directly in front of me and opens the robe like a flasher. She *is* naked and magnificent. She brings her boobs up to my cock and squeezes them together around it while she slowly slides up and down. I feel so good and almost instantly five years of passion ejaculates out of me and onto her boobs. She moves up to my face and I suck on her nipples and lick her boobs free of cum.

She stands up, takes my hand and leads me to the bedroom. I lie down on my back while she straddles my face. She tastes every bit as good as I thought she would. I could eat her all day. She squirms, moves and moans as I feel her juices running down the side of my face. She cums with a shudder but I keep going. She lifts herself up just a bit as she gathers herself, then sits back down and I resume eating. Her hand reaches back for my cock which is starting to come back to life. She spins around to the sixty-nine position so she can suck me while I lick her. When I am hard enough she climbs on my cock and starts to ride me. She varies her speed and movements and is breathing hard in no time. I start thrusting along with her and after several minutes she screams in orgasm and I cum along with her.

She slides down next to me on the bed and holds me tight while my fingers fondle her hair. She gently caresses my testicles and as my cock eventually starts to stir she slowly strokes that. When I am almost hard she slides down and takes me in her mouth. She gives me a slow, loving, and absolutely incredible blowjob. I cum in her mouth; she swallows and moves back up and puts her head on my chest. We lie there a long time without saying a word – we don't need to. We are both feeling that sense of intimacy we have been missing for such a long time and it is the greatest feeling in the world.

Paddles

Walking through the parking lot, she reflected on what had been a very stressful workday. She got in her car but rather than start it right away she closed her eyes and drew a deep breath, holding it for a moment before slowly exhaling. The next part of her day should be much more interesting and, hopefully, a lot of fun.

The address had already been entered into her GPS; it was only a few minutes away. She found the house easily and parked in the driveway – right on time. She paused and again closed her eyes to visualize what would happen. She met this guy in her social group and they seemed to hit it off but they had never 'played' together. She got out of the car but stood there for a moment to get into character, then walked up to the door and rang the bell.

He opened the door a few seconds later. Smiling at her, he said, "Hi, come on in."

Without saying a word, she walked through the short entryway and into the living room. She quickly took in the surroundings. Open floor plan with the living, dining, and kitchen areas all connected. The stone fireplace was directly ahead, the vaulted ceilings with two skylights gave the room an open and airy feel. There was leather furniture with a low coffee table and plenty of space. This would do nicely.

She reached the center of the room and turned to face him. Her legs were spread slightly apart, hands on hips, and a stern expression on her face. The smile had left his as he looked at her, seemingly unsure of what to do next.

"You know why I'm here, so let's get on with it."

His mouth dropped open in surprise but he just stood there.

"Drop em!"

He started fumbling for his belt and nervously opened his jeans and dropped them so that they bunched around his ankles.

She shook her head. "Are you some kind of prude? The underwear too!"

He quickly yanked down his briefs and they joined his jeans near the floor. She looked at his crotch and saw his penis start to grow, quickly becoming fully erect.

She moved in closer. "Are you kidding me? You've got a freekin' hard-on? I'm not here to fuck you!"

As she said it she gave his penis a hard slap with her open hand and in one motion returned in the opposite direction and sharply smacked his testicles with the back of her hand. He cried out sharply in obvious discomfort as his erection slowly subsided.

She was about an arm's length away as she slowly walked in a circle around him. His head turned as he tried to follow her with his eyes.

"Look straight ahead. Focus on the clock on the mantle and nothing else. Do you understand?"

"Yes"

"Yes what?"

"Yes, ma'am."

"That's better."

She circled him several times checking him out. She lightly caressed his buttocks and noticed a slight stirring of the penis. At that point she grabbed one of his butt cheeks with her right hand and squeezed until he winced – the stirring quickly stopped. It was time.

Leaving him standing there, she moved to the dining table and moved a heavy wooden chair to the center of the room. She sat down and motioned for him to sit across her lap by patting on her legs. He moved toward her and positioned himself across her lap. His pants were still tangled around his ankles and the palms of his hands were flat against the floor.

She started by gently caressing his ass cheeks one at a time. She gave a soft smack and caressed some more. She then spanked several times in succession – *whack, whack, whack.* She paused and lightly ran her fingertips up and down his inner thighs before bringing her hand down sharply again – *whack, whack, whack.* She repeated this for several minutes alternating between soft touches and hard smacks but increasing the intensity of the spanks until his ass was glowing red.

By this time she had need at it for almost twenty minutes and her hand was tired and getting a bit sore so she nudged him to indicate that he should get up. He did so but she wasn't done.

"Remove your clothes – all of them."

He dutifully stepped out the bunched up bundle around his ankles, removed is socks, and took off his shirt. He stood there completely naked. She stood up and circled him again, gently patting his now-red cheeks.

She motioned toward the kitchen peninsula. "Brace yourself against the counter."

As he did so she picked up a paddle that had been waiting on the coffee table. She walked up behind him and pushed on his back so he leaned forward. Using her foot she nudged his ankles so that he spread his legs further apart until he was positioned just right.

She could sense his nervous anticipation. She also noticed the erection was back but this time she ignored it. She used the edge of the paddle to gently trace the inside of his thighs, just as her fingers had done. She lightly ran the paddle of his cheeks before giving a light tap. She continued the process, increasing the intensity of the paddle strokes each time until she was hitting him fairly hard. She could see by the deepening redness that bruises would soon form so she figured that was enough.

She reached for a tube of lotion that was sitting on the counter. She squeezed a generous amount on her hand and spread it on his cheeks. She could feel the heat from his ass as it radiated on to her hand.

She smiled for the first time. "What do you say?"

"Thank you."

"Thank you, what?"

"Thank you ma'am."

"That's better. Now get us a glass of wine."

He started to reach for his clothes.

"Leave them off; I want to admire my handiwork."

She watched his red cheeks with amusement as he walked into the kitchen to do as she asked. He returned a moment later with two glasses of red wine and sat down in the chair across from her, still naked.

She sipped her wine. "Now tell me about the first time a woman spanked you."

He began telling her the story in a very animated manner – his erection was back.

The Specimen

Ms. Atwood looked at her clipboard. "Bring in the subject."

Kerri brought in a middle-aged man, approximately 6'1" and 190 pounds, wearing a polo shirt and khaki pants. She led him to the center of the room and had him stand on "feet" marks painted on the floor. She quietly instructed him to stand up straight, remain silent, and focus his gaze on a picture on the far wall at all times. He nodded in understanding and assumed his position as instructed. Kerri returned to her place at Ms. Atwood's right, standing slightly behind her mentor.

Today's class focused on domination role play in a medical setting. Playing her part as a medical assistant trainee would be easy since that precisely described her. Atwood stepped forward and visually examined the subject from head to toe, front and back, and each side. Kerri followed closely and mimicked her mentor, though she didn't understand what she was looking for, or if it even mattered. After circling the man several times, Atwood returned to her previous position and Kerri followed.

"Lower the trousers."

Kerri stepped forward and moved directly in front of their specimen. She looked at his faced and could tell he was struggling to maintain his focus on the far wall. She saw his Adam's apple bob as she dropped into a crouch and began to unbuckle his belt. She lowered the zipper after unfastening the button. Remembering her mentor's instruction, she lowered the pants slowly in order to tease him. That task accomplished, her fingers grasped the band of his briefs alongside his hips. Her face was less than a foot from his crotch and his penis, now starting to grow erect, seemed to jump at her as she pulled his underwear down. She did her best not to react as she lowered his briefs until they met his trousers. She stood up and backed away, her subject's pants bunched up around his ankles – a situation that, according to her mentor, would create a feeling of extreme vulnerability in their specimen.

Kerri took her position at Ms. Atwood's side. They both stared at the man without making a sound. They maintained that posture for more than two minutes; Kerri felt discomfort at the silence, she could only imagine how their subject felt. Finally Atwood broke the spell by scribbling something on her clipboard.

'Tell me what you observe; what's the first thing you notice?"

Kerri's eyes dropped to the man's crotch. "He doesn't shave his pubic hair."

"Pretty obvious," Atwood remarked. "Why might that be? What does it tell you about our subject?"

Kerri cocked her head. "He's not well groomed?"

Atwood snickered. "You're so young. It may be hard for you to believe, but there was a time when people didn't shave there. Even harder to imagine perhaps is that some people, often older, prefer pubic hair. Look at the rest of him – the hair on his head is nicely cut and his goatee is neatly trimmed."

Kerri was puzzled. "So what *does* his pubic hair tell us?"

"To me it indicates that our subject is a traditionalist who does not follow the latest fad. If he were allowed to speak I wager that he'd tell us he prefers pubic hair on women."

"*Really?*" Kerri noticed the muscles on their subject's face strain as he struggled to suppress a smile.

Atwood glanced at her clipboard. "What else do you see?"

"He's circumcised."

"Good, what else do you notice?"

Kerri smiled. "He started to get hard but now seems to have gone back down."

"Some initial arousal is not unexpected. What about the penis?"

"Well, he seems larger than average, though not huge."

Atwood jotted something down. "Perhaps, but I'm more concerned with details. Step closer."

They moved in until they were inches away. The man's eyes followed them briefly before returning to the wall. Atwood threw a stern glance in his direction and the man gulped. Her mentor stared directly into his face as her right hand cupped his balls and kneaded them very lightly. She sensed, rather than saw, the subject's tension.

Atwood kept staring into the man's eyes. "Take note of the testicles – you feel them."

Kerri felt the man's balls and tried to fondle them the way Atwood had.

"Notice how one hangs lower than the other? See how loose they feel? When a man is ready to ejaculate they tighten up and move closer to the body – a handy warning sign."

Kerri released the man's jewels. Her mentor had squatted down in front of the subject's penis, so she did the same. He was starting to become erect again. She could only imagine how he felt having two woman hovering inches from his cock; after all, she herself was feeling aroused as she realized he was larger than she initially thought. Atwood did not seem impressed, though in her role she shouldn't be.

Atwood's fingers grabbed the tip of the man's cock as she manipulated it. "Notice the penis; it's easier to see the features now that he's hard. See how the head is a different color? Do you see the band around the middle of the shaft?"

The man's penis, now fully erect, seemed to throb as she watched Atwood examine it. At her mentor's urging, she took the subject's penis in her left hand and held it as the fingers of her right lightly traced its features.

"You mean this part here?"

"Precisely. That portion between the band and the head is more sensitive than the rest. What do you think that means?"

Kerri knew the answer to this. "That's where I should focus if I want to make a man feel good."

"True, if you're performing fellatio of example, run your tongue over that sensitive area intermittently to produce the desired results. However, you can also use that knowledge to tease the individual."

Kerri noticed a drop of fluid on the tip of the penis. "Is he ejaculating?"

Atwood touched the fluid and rubbed it between her fingers. "No, that's pre-cum – it's part of the arousal process."

Atwood returned to her position so Kerri followed suit and stood slightly behind her. They once again stood silently as they observed their subject. Almost immediately the man's penis began to deflate, though she sensed his struggle to maintain his position. Kerri was impressed by his ability to maintain his posture, though he had flinched noticeably a couple of times. His greatest difficulty seemed to be staying focused on the wall; she caught his eyes wandering to look at her on several occasions and assumed her mentor had noticed as well. Just as the silence reached an almost unbearable level, Atwood looked to her clipboard.

"How do you think our specimen performed?"

Kerri paused a moment before speaking. "He flinched a few times but remained silent. All told, I think he did well."

"You may have missed a few things. The flinching wasn't bad, but he did moan slightly when you touched his penis. He also failed to maintain eye discipline."

"But only a couple of times," Kerri said in the man's defense.

Atwood glanced toward her. "You obviously did not see the eyes following you."

"I guess not. What do we do now?"

"Remove your shorts."

Kerri hesitated, but only for a moment. She unfastened her shorts and let them drop to the floor before kicking them aside. As she stood there in her g-string their subject's erection instantly returned.

Atwood snickered again. "Just as I suspected."

Kerri maintained her position while Atwood left the room only to return a moment later with a straight-back chair, placing it between her and their subject. After adjusting the chair's position to her liking, Atwood resumed her position.

Kerri was puzzled. "Now what?"

"The specimen failed to follow instructions, so discipline must be imposed. Go sit in the chair."

Kerri did as she was told and sat in the chair. Her mentor adjusted her position before moving to the man. Atwood's hand seized the subject by his still-erect penis and led him toward the side of the chair. Her free hand pushed on his back as the penis-clutching hand pulled him down until he was lying across Kerri's lap. Kerri experienced a jolt of sexual electricity when she felt the erect cock on her bare thigh.

"Spank him."

Kerri raised her hand and brought it down on the man's ass. *Slap.* She lifted and struck the other cheek. *Slap.* She repeated the process, pausing between each strike. *Slap…slap….slap.*

Atwood shook her head. "Be forceful, little love taps like that will not have the desired effect. Do it harder."

Kerri paused and gritted her teeth. She raised her hand and brought it down as hard as she could. *Smack.* The man twitched a little but it seemed to hurt her more than it did him. *Smack….smack….smack.*

Atwood touched Kerri's shoulder indicating that she should stop. Though her hand hurt, the man's ass was only slightly pink – and he was still erect. Her mentor pulled on the man's shoulder and had him stand up before motioning for Kerri to do the same. Atwood sat in the chair and pulled the man down across her lap. Kerri noticed his erection had subsided and there was apprehension in his eyes.

Her mentor shrugged her shoulders and raised her hand. "Pay close attention."

Whack…whack….whack….whack.

"Ow! Oh, shit!"

"Quiet!" *Whack…whack…whack….*

Kerri watched, transfixed as each strike alternated from one cheek to the other. The subject's ass quickly went from pink to red and soon seemed to glow. She saw the man grimace in anticipation of each strike. He exhaled a sigh of relief as Atwood paused, but the respite was short lived.

Whack…whack….whack…

Kerri noticed beads of sweat forming on Atwood's forehead and thought that she would never have the strength to strike someone like that. She no sooner finished that thought when Atwood stopped and had the man stand up before getting up herself. She motioned for Kerri to sit back down and had the man lay across her lap again when she did. She felt the heat when her hand touched their subject's ass.

Atwood touched her shoulder and handed her something. "This should make it easier for you."

Kerri accepted the paddle and looked at it briefly, turning it in her hand and assessing its weight. She raised it and brought it down on the glowing, red flesh. *Whack!* "Now that's more like it!" *Whack….whack….whack…*

After several minutes Atwood touched Kerri's shoulder indicating it was time to stop. Kerri felt the sweat on her brow but her hand didn't hurt. Their subject returned to his position and did his best to stand straight. His face covered in sweat, his eyes moist, and his erection long gone, he seemed suitably chastised. Kerri returned to her position just behind her mentor.

Atwood smiled for the first time. "I think our specimen has been sufficiently admonished."

Kerri smiled. "I should say so. What now?"

Atwood handed her a small dish. "It's time for you to collect a semen sample."

Kerri accepted the plate with a smile as she watched the man's erection begin to return.

The Dare

Sitting on the barstool, Katie reflected on how things had escalated. What started as a simple exchange of sexual dares had reached a point she never considered possible, nor did she realize how much it would terrify and excite her at the same time. She didn't blame Derrick because, not only had she started it all, she had encouraged him to push it. So here she sat her heart racing in terror while her crotch tingled with anticipation.

She took a sip from the chocolate martini in front of her as she glanced at Derrick sitting beside her. He was scanning the room with a gleeful look on his face. Was he really going to make her do this? She knew he was and she had no one to blame but herself. Her mind wandered to how this had started.

Everything began as a simple power exchange arrangement in the bedroom. They took turns switching roles; one day he was in charge and the next she would lead their erotic activities. It encouraged them to experiment and push their sexual boundaries. They set very loose limits – no blood or poop – other than that they would not refuse each other. They would, however, have a debriefing after each session and either agree to include something in their future repertoire or eliminate it forever. Thus, there would only be one golden shower in her life. Things really changed when it left the bedroom.

It was a beautiful spring day and they were walking through a local park, something they did often. They chatted as they strolled, discussing fairly mundane things until they started exchanging ideas for sex play. He mentioned the possibility of her having a wardrobe malfunction and 'accidentally' exposing a nipple in public. They considered possible locations such as a restaurant, supermarket, or store in a mall. She was intrigued by the idea but came up with what she thought was an even better one.

She looked at him and smiled. "Take your dick out."

He looked at her in surprise. "What?"

"You can have a malfunction too; take your dick out."

"I can't do that here."

"Sure you can. The bathroom is just up ahead. Go in and come out like you forgot to put it away."

"But..."

"Besides," she said with a laugh, "it's my turn – do it!"

"Yes ma'am."

She waited outside of the restroom, laughing at his discomfort. He came out a couple of minutes later with his penis dangling from his shorts as ordered. He was not exactly small so it would be difficult to miss. They ambled along hand-in-hand passing a number of people, mostly couples along with an occasional jogger. While no one said anything, they surely noticed. She could hear people whispering to each other with some laughs and giggles mixed in. She was certainly amused. When they got back to the car and started discussing it she knew his exhibitionist jaunt excited him because he was instantly erect. She rewarded him right there with a blow job. His excitement was confirmed when he exploded in her mouth almost instantly.

The public play continued. She had a few malfunctions of her own exposing herself at a few different locations, most commonly allowing waiters and an interested waitress or two have quite an eyeful. They were becoming comfortable with the public play and, once again, it was she who pushed it further. They were back in the park one morning and walked toward an area with picnic tables, though the area was deserted at this time. She sat on one of the tables and he was about to join her but she stopped him.

"Stand there and drop your pants."

Derrick glanced around to be sure no one was around and did as she asked. He would certainly be visible to anyone who walked by.

"Now look at me and jerk off."

"But what if someone sees me?"

"They'll get a show."

"I could get arrested."

"I'll bail you out."

He stood about five feet away from her. Her back was to the walking path as he began stroking himself. She could tell her was nervous but he masturbated to a fairly quick orgasm, ejaculating a nice stream that shot in her direction but fell far short of hitting her. When they discussed it afterward he didn't have any objection so it was added to their repertoire. What she did not realize was how much further this would push their game.

She sat at the bar, her martini almost gone when another appeared in front of her. She looked at Derrick as he sipped his second beer. This was taking things to another level entirely and she could have refused the moment he suggested it. However, the thought of it excited her and in the last week she had masturbated several times thinking about. But now the moment was here and she was terrified.

She looked into his excited eyes. "The first one?"

"Yes, the first guy who walks in alone."

"What if he's young? Why would he want a forty-year-old woman?"

"You're forty-two."

"Fuck you!"

Derrick laughed. "Besides, you are in your prime cougar-hood; young guys like that."

"But I'm fat."

"You're not fat; you're just a little 'squishy' and you have killer boobs."

She smiled at the last comment and she was showing plenty of cleavage. Just then a guy walked in by himself. He was about thirty and hot; her heart skipped a beat. Unfortunately a woman joined him a few seconds later. She was inwardly relieved.

She looked at Derrick again. "I have to say it just like that?"

"Exactly like that."

"What if he says 'no'?"

He shook his head. "He won't, but if he does you're off the hook."

Just then a man of about forty walked in. He had an average build and was not bad looking at all. Her heart started racing again.

Derrick pushed her gently. "Go get him."

She took a deep breath and got up off the stool. She walked over to the man and intercepted him before he could make his way to the bar. She smiled at him and he smiled back as she approached.

She stuck out her hand to shake and he took it. "Hi, I'm Katie and I want to suck your cock while my husband watches."

The guy didn't even seem surprised and quickly responded, "Let's do it!"

The three of them went out to her car. Derrick sat in the front while she got into the back with the guy. She started fumbling with his belt and zipper; he helped and yanked his pants down exposing a nice package that was already erect. She took a good look at it before taking it in her mouth. It was the first penis she had touched since before she was dating Derrick almost fifteen years ago. She took her time and savored every moment. After a few minutes he started breathing heavily and grunted rewarding her with a nice load which she swallowed.

As the guy caught his breath Katie said, "I'm sorry, I didn't get your name."

Derrick chimed in, "That's Harold; he works out with me at the gym."

Stunned, Katie turn to him. "You set this up?"

"Yup"

"You bastard! I'll get you for this!"

"Oh, I hope you do…I hope you do."

About the Author

J.W. Richard is a freelance journalist and a graduate of the University of Nevada Las Vegas. Originally from New York, J.W. currently resides in North Carolina.

www.ingramcontent.com/pod-product-compliance
Lightning Source LLC
Chambersburg PA
CBHW052007150726
47999CB00004B/1565